Secrets of a Soccer Mom

by

Kathleen Clark

SAMUEL FRENCH

FOUNDED 1830

NEW YORK HOLLYWOOD LONDON TORONTO

SAMUELFRENCH.COM

ISBN 978-0-573-66395-6   Printed in U.S.A.   #21486

IMPORTANT BILLING AND CREDIT
REQUIREMENTS

All producers of *SECRETS OF A SOCCER MOM must* give credit to the Author of the Play in all programs distributed in connection with performances of the Play, and in all instances in which the title of the Play appears for the purposes of advertising, publicizing or otherwise exploiting the Play and/or a production. The name of the Author *must* appear on a separate line on which no other name appears, immediately following the title and *must* appear in size of type not less than fifty percent of the size of the title type.

SECRETS OF A SOCCER MOM opened off-Broadway at the Snapple Theater Center on March 5, 2008. It was produced by A-Frame Productions with direction by Judith Ivey, set design by Lex Liang, lighting design by Jeff Croiter, costume design by Elizabeth Flauto and sound design by Zachary Williamson. The cast was as follows:

NANCY . . . . Nancy Ringham

LYNN . . . . Deborah Sonnenberg

ALISON . . . . Caralyn Kozlowski

(Originally produced as "Soccer Moms" at Fleetwood Stage Company in New Rochelle, New York)

CHARACTERS

ALISON - Twenties, has a husband, Ron, a son, Aaron, and a daughter, Adele

LYNN - Thirties, has a husband, Lennie, a son, Larry, and twin daughters

NANCY - Forties, has a husband, Kevin, a son, Jack, and a daughter, Sally

PLACE AND TIME

A soccer field on a Sunday

THE SET

The set is stylized with touches of realism. A rectangular painting of sky and clouds hangs upstage. The sky and clouds look real; the deep blue sky background and white, puffy clouds are similar to those seen in the painting *Ecstasy* by Maxfield Parrish. If desired, autumn leaves can be painted on the canvas or scattered in different parts of the set. One or two benches, or short bleachers, face the audience.

THE OFFSTAGE WORLD

The device, of the three women watching the field, the parking lot and all offstage areas, works best if all areas are clearly defined by the actors. The offstage soccer goals for each side must be determined as well as where each off stage character is located. When the actors talk to an off stage character it must either be to the field which is over the heads of the audience, or to the parking lot and tree, stage left and stage right. They should not talk upstage toward the sky. In the script, lines said to offstage characters are in caps. Everything offstage should be left to the imagination of the audience.

THE SOUNDS

The play was written to be performed with a bare number of sounds: the music played during the prologue and at the end of the play, referee whistles, the sound of a boy's voice yelling, "Mom" at the end of the prologue and the sound of a child crying loudly at the beginning of scene five. (If music is desired during the playing of the game in scene five, it should be something noble and not a traditional sports song.)

If more sound is desired, it's possible to add various offstage sounds of dogs barking, horns blowing, etc. as long as these sounds do not become disruptive or distracting to the three characters and their stories.

THE INTERRUPTIONS OFFSTAGE

When the women are yelling to their children, either reprimanding or guiding, the interruption does not always change their tone of voice when they resume speaking. Sometimes they interrupt themselves to yell and immediately return to the tone of voice they had before the interruption. The change of focus becomes as natural and expected to the women as breathing.

THE PROLOGUE

During the prologue, there are three circles of light where the three women stand. They are working seriously and only gradually, as they get into the music, do they start their passionate dancing. We must see the journey from bored to wild dancing to standing frozen at the sound of "Mom" being yelled at them.

THE GAME AT THE END

The three women are back in their original spots for the game. They look straight ahead and don't turn to look at one another as they play and talk. They mime their actions in one place without moving around the stage.

PROLOGUE

(Three women stand in three separate spotlights. Next to each woman is a small table with a different type of radio on each table.)

(NANCY, a woman in her forties, has a basket of clean clothes in front of her. She turns on the radio as she folds the clothes. The song she hears should be a rock and roll anthem that inspires fast dancing and is a tribute to youth and freedom, similar to "Glory Days" by Bruce Springsteen, "Man! I Feel like a Woman!" by Shania Twain or "Think" by Aretha Franklin. NANCY moves her head to the music as she folds.)

(LYNN, a woman in her thirties, is working on sorting envelopes, order forms and little golden books. She uses a magic marker to write on the envelopes. She clicks on the radio and hears the same song. She mouths the words as she works.)

(ALISON, a woman in her twenties, is packing clothes into a suitcase. As she does this, she, too, turns on the radio and starts to sway with the music.)

(As the music gets faster, the three dance faster, moving with the music, until they are dancing wildly, passionately, eyes closed. NANCY twirls laundry above her head. LYNN uses her marker as a microphone. ALISON dances with a sexy nightgown. At their most abandoned moment, we hear a loud eight year old voice yell, "MOM, COME ON!" The women freeze, the music stops and the lights go out.)

Scene One

(Lights up on one or two benches and a rectangle canvas hanging upstage. The rectangle has a deep blue sky and white clouds painted on it; the clouds are similar to those in a Maxfield Parrish painting, specifically "Ecstasy." Brightly colored autumn leaves are placed around the set.)

(The sound of a whistle. **ALISON** *and* **LYNN** *enter, running to the bench.* **LYNN** *bends over, breathing heavily, trying to get her breath.* **ALISON** *checks her pulse, not as winded.)*

ALISON. Boy, they're playing rough...the size of some of them!

LYNN. I can't breathe.

*(***NANCY*** *enters, slowly, staggering. She is dressed in layers, like* **LYNN** *and* **ALISON***, to keep warm.)*

NANCY. I so don't want to be here.

LYNN. When...I...was...just guarding...you know...not running, I was kind of okay...but...the...running up and down the field...all that running...couldn't stop or... get run over...

ALISON. I'm kind of getting into it.

LYNN. No kidding, you almost ran me over.

ALISON. I'm sorry, but you sat down right in the middle of the field.

NANCY. And Gloria got hit by that ball you kicked at her.

ALISON. I didn't kick it at her, I was passing it to her. She shouldn't have covered her eyes. She was in a position to score.

NANCY. Score? What are you talking about, score. We're playing eight year olds. You don't think we're out there to win, do you?

ALISON. We're not?

NANCY. No. Are you?

ALISON. I didn't think about it. Once I got out there, it just seemed natural to...Lynn, is that why you were sitting down?

LYNN. I was sitting down because I couldn't breathe. So, what are you saying, Nancy, we let them win?

NANCY. Ssssshhh. Of course we let them win, what did you think?

ALISON. So what do we do, just stand there?

NANCY. No, no, not so it's obvious. When we were out there I saw how easy it was to kick it just to the side of the net or look like you're trying to stop their goal, but then let it go in.

LYNN. Why didn't I think of this? Larry's team hasn't won a game all year. He'll love it.

ALISON. So we play, but we play badly. Is that what you mean?

LYNN. Maybe we should get one goal later so they don't catch on. Look,there goes team B for round two. LARRY, LEAVE THE BUTTERFLY ALONE, YOUR COACH IS CALLING YOU!

(**ALISON** *exits.*)

NANCY. (*nods toward* **ALISON**) Well! She's a little intense, isn't she?

LYNN. She's okay.

NANCY. I guess, but she's always trying to corner me after school to talk – even when I'm hiding in the car, trying to read the newspaper, she finds me and taps on the window, "Nancy, Nancy..."

(**ALISON** *enters.*)

ALISON. So, that's it. We're really going to throw the game.

NANCY. (*laughs*) Throw the game. This is just about the kids having fun, not us going for the gold.

ALISON. I know I'm new here, but still, I thought it was suppose to be a real game.

LYNN. Come on, Alison, they'll jump around and high five each other and feel good about themselves.

NANCY. It's just a way of doing something nice for your son.

ALISON. By pretending that I don't know how to kick a ball down a field? I'm a lousy mother if I play well?

NANCY. You're looking at it all wrong. We're just trying to do what's best for the kids. That's all I want.

ALISON. Well, so do I.

NANCY. So then what's the problem?

ALISON. It's not a problem. All I'm trying to say is…well, it's just that when I got possession of the ball and started running toward the goal…

LYNN. Got possession? Alison, this is Sunday afternoon kick the ball around, not the Super Bowl.

ALISON. It's just that…

NANCY. *(impatiently)* What? It's just what?

(**NANCY** *and* **LYNN** *look at* **ALISON**.)

ALISON. Nothing. Whatever you guys want.

NANCY. I mean, really, what difference does it make?

ALISON. I said okay.

NANCY. No, I want to know.

LYNN. Nancy, she said okay. Come on, we better tell Jane and her group. They look pretty serious out there.

ALISON. Maybe they won't want to do it.

NANCY. *(incredulous)* You mean they might prefer to crush their sons in a soccer game?

ALISON. Obviously not crush them, but play the game.

LYNN. Look, we have to tell the others…

NANCY. So what's it going to be?

(*pause*)

ALISON. *(reluctantly)* All right. They win.

NANCY. Good.

(*Everything suddenly gets very dark. The three women look up.*)

ALISON. God, it's like all the lights went out.

NANCY. It's just that one single black cloud that's moving across the sun. Look at it.

(NANCY walks slowly off stage, looking up at the sun.)

LYNN. NANCY! LOOK OUT!

NANCY. *(offstage)* OUCH!

(LYNN and ALISON gasp.)

(BLACK OUT)

End of Scene One

Scene Two

(Lights up on NANCY *holding an icepack to her forehead.*
ALISON *and* LYNN *huddle around her, concerned.)*

LYNN. Are you sure you're all right?

NANCY. It was so sudden, you know? Like one minute I'm looking up at the sun and the next I'm on the ground.

ALISON. You have the imprint of the ball on your fore-head.

LYNN. That's just dirt, it doesn't say 'Wilson' or anything.

*(*LYNN *wipes the dirt off* NANCY*'s head.)*

LYNN. Gordon kicked it. He said he was sorry.

ALISON. Yeah and then he said did you see how hard I kicked that ball?

NANCY. That sounds more like Gordon. Boy, you never know what's coming at you. I should walk around a little, just in case Jack's watching. I don't want him to think I'm hurt.

*(*NANCY *paces rapidly, holding her head.)*

Who's out there now, still team B?

LYNN. Looks like it.

NANCY. *(pointing toward field, nudges* LYNN*)* GOOD KICK, LARRY!

LYNN. *(not seeing her son, looks in all directions, clapping)* Oh, yeah…GOOD KICK, HONEY! Oh, Nancy, look at Jane. Look how fast she's running!

NANCY. Must be left over aggression from her lawyer days. WHOA, JANE…NICE SAVE!

ALISON. I thought you said…

NANCY. No, I mean, what's she doing, we have to go easy on them.

ALISON. So, Lynn, we don't play again until B,C and D teams play, right?

LYNN. That's right, like the boys, everybody plays in shifts. So make yourself comfortable.

ALISON. AARON! REMEMBER WHAT I SAID ABOUT USING THE INSIDE OF YOUR FOOT!

(NANCY *watches* LYNN *as she pulls out envelopes, books, P.T.A. work from her canvas bag and sets up an organized work area, possibly using a garbage can as a desk.* NANCY *takes her 35 mm camera out of her bag.*)

NANCY. Don't tell me you carry P.T.A. work around with you in case you get an extra minute.

LYNN. All right, I won't.

NANCY. JANE! I WANT TO TALK TO YOU. I'll be right back, I have to straighten these girls out. She almost scored.

(NANCY *exits.* ALISON *takes a thick book out of her duffel bag and puts it on the bench.*)

ALISON. So…what'd the doctor say about the twins?

LYNN. This week it's ear infections – four ears, four infections. We see the pediatrician so much, I'm considering refinishing the attic so I can move him in full-time.

ALISON. So they're okay?

LYNN. They're fine, they're on amoxicillin. I'd never heard of it before, now I can spell it.

ALISON. Is your husband coming? He seemed very nice the other day when I met him.

LYNN. He is nice. He's bringing the twins. Is yours?

ALISON. Nice? Well, uh…sometimes…No, I guess not…

LYNN. No, no, I mean is he coming?

ALISON. Oh! Yeah, later. I thought you meant…

(*A cell phone rings.* ALISON *and* LYNN *both search their bags.* ALISON *answers.* LYNN *goes back to work.* ALISON *walks away, talking quietly into the phone. She moves around, trying to get better reception.*)

ALISON. Hello?…Can you hear me?…Can you hear me now?…Oh hi, I was going to call you…I want you to wait until Ron goes to work before you come on

Tuesday. What?…Oh no…that's awful…You're still coming, aren't you?…

(sighs deeply)

No, of course I don't want my kids exposed. Hope he feels better. All right.I'll talk to you next week. Bye.

(She hangs up.)

Damn it.

LYNN. What's the matter?

ALISON. Someone was going to watch my kids for me, but her son's got the chicken pox.

*(**ALISON** exits, running.)*

LYNN. Chicken pox? She's not from town, is she? Alison?

*(**LYNN** looks around and doesn't see **ALISON**. Suddenly, **ALISON** runs back as quickly as she left.)*

LYNN. What are you doing?

ALISON. I have to keep checking on Adele. I left her asleep in the car.

*(**ALISON** studies **LYNN**.)*

Lynn.

*(**LYNN**, back at work,doesn't look up.)*

LYNN. Hmmmm?

ALISON. Do you think you could watch my kids for me?

LYNN. Sure. When?

ALISON. Next week.

LYNN. What day next week?

ALISON. The whole week.

LYNN. The whole week? Are you kidding?

ALISON. No. No, I'm not.

LYNN. I don't know. Gosh. Where are you going?

ALISON. AARON, RUN THE OTHER WAY. THAT'S THE WRONG GOAL! It's hard to talk about – I get very emotional.

LYNN. Are you all right?

ALISON. Well, not really. Oh, you mean physically…it's not that, I'm not sick. I have to go away.

LYNN. Gosh, Alison, a week…I mean, a week?

ALISON. I wouldn't ask if I wasn't absolutely desperate.

LYNN. Does it have to be next week? My week is so jammed – a class trip, the bake sale…How about a weekend? Maybe I could do a weekend. Can't you tell me what it's about?

ALISON. Well, it's probably going to sound really crazy. It wasn't clear to me until Friday morning, right after I dropped Aaron…

LYNN. LARRY, STOP DANCING AND PLAY! Sorry, go on…

ALISON. I dropped Aaron and I was walking back to my car and a man, standing behind a truck, looked right at me and said,

(She speaks gruffly, loudly.)

"What'd ya need?" Real rough-like, "What'd ya need?"

LYNN. He said, what do you need?

ALISON. Right and I said, "What do I need?" and he said louder, really demanding, "What'd ya need?" and in that split second it was like a curtain lifted and I saw what I needed. And then I realized he was a construction guy yelling down a hole at another guy. He didn't even know I was there! But in that instant I knew my life had to change and I knew what I had to do.

LYNN. Wow. What?

(NANCY enters, walking backwards, yelling toward the field. ALISON moves away from LYNN.)

NANCY. SO JANE, SPREAD THE WORD, OKAY?

LYNN. What'd they say?

NANCY. A little surprised at first, then, of course, they loved the idea.

(She takes pictures of the game.)

When you think about it, this whole day is pretty absurd. Going out on a field competing against children…

LYNN. As opposed to what – being designated 'Blimpie Lunch Mom' – tell me something that isn't absurd.

NANCY. Blimpie Lunch Mom…never in my wildest dreams…

(**NANCY** *looks toward the field.*)

Talk about absurd. Take a look at the, what do they call them, army fatigue pants, you know the camouflage ones?

LYNN. Where?

NANCY. There. I don't who she is, but, I mean, how does a decision like that get made? You look in your closet and say, hmmmm, should I go with the silk or the army fatigues?

LYNN. Reminds me of a woman I know who wears hiking boots every day – even in the summer. She used to do a lot of back-packing. So I'm thinking maybe she wears them to remember who she was…

NANCY. So what's this one trying to remember, combat?

ALISON. Maybe she's trying to camouflage herself from being a mom.

NANCY. Good luck with that.

LYNN. Oh. Hey, Nance, I have two words for you.

NANCY. What.

LYNN. Bronx Zoo.

NANCY. Yeah, well, I have two words for you too.

LYNN. Charming. Why am I not surprised?

NANCY. What do you mean?

LYNN. Forget it.

(**ALISON** *suddenly runs off, exiting.*)

NANCY. Where's she going?

LYNN. Her daughter's sleeping in the car.

NANCY. Did you hear her get on me about the game? I hope she lightens up out there. I can just hear the boys if they lose to their mothers.

LYNN. Well, wait til you hear this. She wants me to watch her kids…

NANCY. So?

LYNN. For a week!

NANCY. A week? My God. I can't imagine leaving my kids for a week. Why?

LYNN. She's going "away"…

NANCY. What do you mean "away"? Where?

LYNN. She won't say.

NANCY. She didn't say or she won't say?

LYNN. She won't say. She said she gets emotional when she talks about it.

NANCY. Is she sick?

LYNN. No. I asked her, it's not that. Something to do with a construction guy yelling at her.

NANCY. A construction guy?

LYNN. That part's a little fuzzy. She wants to change her life.

NANCY. Change her life. Wonder what it could be.

LYNN. Well, it could be…never mind.

NANCY. What?

LYNN. I was told not to repeat it.

NANCY. By Alison?

LYNN. No, someone in the park last week.

NANCY. Who?

LYNN. I can't remember her name.

NANCY. Look, Lynn, I just made up a new park rule. If you don't remember a woman's name you don't have to keep her secrets. Now come on, I never talk to anyone but you anyway, who am I going to tell?

LYNN. All right.

(**LYNN** *looks around and then whispers to* **NANCY**.)

I'm guessing it's about her husband.

NANCY. (*mocking* **LYNN**, *looking around and whispering*) What about her husband?

LYNN. I heard he's fooling around.

NANCY. How do people find these things out? I'm serious. How does the woman in the park know that?

LYNN. Don't ask me, I'm just telling you what I heard. And you didn't hear it from me. Look, Kevin and Sally just got here.

NANCY. KEVIN, HOW'S SALLY?…She fell this morning… SHE'S OKAY? THAT'S A RELIEF. SEE YOU LATER. What a day…

(She rubs her head.)

I still can't believe it, can you?

LYNN. It could happen to anybody.

NANCY. Sure, I guess, if you're not looking.

LYNN. Sometimes even if you're looking. My roommate from college. Right under her nose. She was in shock.

NANCY. Under her nose? In her mouth, you mean?

LYNN. What? Under her nose, you know, behind her back.

NANCY. Which is it, her nose or her back? What are you talking about?

LYNN. Cheating husbands. What are you talking about?

NANCY. Getting knocked over! The ball in my head.

LYNN. Ohhhh. You're still on that? I'm talking about Alison and her husband.

NANCY. Ohhh. No, no. Me. Me getting knocked over. I just didn't see it…You know that feeling? When you get blindsided by something that you didn't see coming? I went from being fine to being on the ground.

LYNN. You seem fine.

NANCY. I'm not fine. I got knocked down!

LYNN. Why don't you help me with this stuff? Get your mind off it.

NANCY. I mean I didn't wake up thinking I better brace myself in case I get knocked to the ground by a soccer ball today. It's disconcerting, that's what it is.

LYNN. *(softly)* Yeah, yeah. Disconcerting. Always something.

NANCY. You could be a little more sympathetic.

LYNN. Come on, help me.

NANCY. KEVIN, WHAT'D YOU SAY? YES, I DID – RIGHT IN THE HEAD. IT'S NOTHING. I FORGOT ALL ABOUT IT!

(**LYNN** *looks at her in disbelief and shakes her head.*)

NANCY. HEY, THERE GOES SALLY! He didn't want to watch Sally during our game…

(*She shields her eyes, watching Kevin.*)

Running a company he can do with his eyes closed, playing Barbie is unimaginable.

LYNN. You ask him to play Barbie?

NANCY. I play Barbie, why can't he? What's hard? You pick up a doll and say, "Hi, I'm Barbie, want to go to the movies with me?" and then she picks up her doll and says, "Sure, let's go." Why is that such a hard concept? Actually, I like playing Barbie because I live vicariously through her adventures – Barbie being doctor, the new Barbie as president…I especially like going dancing with the hip hop Ken doll.

(**ALISON** *runs back on.*)

ALISON. Adele's still asleep, thank God. Ron was suppose to watch her, but he had to go into the office…

LYNN. (*raises her eyes suspiciously*) On Sunday?

ALISON. This day's so important to me and as usual he's somewhere else. I left him a note to come over as soon as he gets home.

NANCY. Important? Playing soccer?

(**NANCY** *and* **LYNN** *exchange looks.*)

NANCY. JACK, GET OUT OF THAT TREE! THANK YOU.

ALISON. (*looks toward the field, smiles and waves*) HI! HOW ARE YOU? See that guy over there?

LYNN. The young guy from the grocery store?

ALISON. Yeah. I was there the other day, kidding around with him while he stocking shelves. Anyway, a woman walks by, yelling at her kids and he says, "Mothers scare me" and we laugh. So the next day I go in with Aaron and I'm yelling at him to stop loading the buggy with cookies when that guy comes around the corner. I can tell he's happy to see me by his big smile. Then he sees my face, tight and angry, saying through clenched teeth, "Put them back right now." His smile disappears, he backs up and in an instant he's gone. It never occurred to me he meant me – that I've become scary.

LYNN. *(wistfully)* It is sad, isn't it? That we have to say good by to that lighthearted girl who used to be.

NANCY. *(impatiently)* What choice do you have? My kids don't want me to be, what, flirty? Ha! They'd hate that. Hmmm, lighthearted. Now that reminds me of...JACK! PUT SALLY DOWN, YOU'RE GOING TO DROP HER!...wait yes, something's coming back to me...it reminds me of...hold on, yes, I've got it.

LYNN. What?

NANCY. A thought.

(pause)

...DON'T MAKE ME COME OVER THERE.

ALISON. What is it?

NANCY. He's going to drop her.

ALISON. No, no, your thought.

NANCY. Too late, it's gone.

ALISON. Was it something about lighthearted?

NANCY. I don't know. Oh, it was...St. Martin...that's it...

LYNN. The island?

ALISON. What about it?

NANCY. JACK! NO!

ALISON. What about St. Martin?

NANCY. What? Not important. Look, who has time to talk to grocery clerks? Or to go away or even think about something else. For me to do this right, I don't have a choice. I am now responsible for keeping two human beings healthy, safe, and happy twenty four hours a day. I mean, what if, right now, he drops her out there and her head splits open? It's so monumental…

(She turns toward Sally and Jack.)

NO, SHE IS NOT HAVING FUN, PUT HER DOWN! And then there's this…How can you even have a coherent conversation with someone if you wanted to? After the word MOM is yelled into your ear thirty two times, how can you possibly know what you were just talking about. Like now, I don't even know what I'm saying… oh no! I knew it. He dropped her. IT'S ALL RIGHT, SALLY, HE DIDN'T MEAN IT. And where'd Kevin go? DON'T CRY, HONEY, I'M COMING.

(NANCY exits. LYNN watches the field, looks at her watch, then pulls out more work from her bag and a cushion. ALISON watches the field.)

ALISON. I like watching Nancy with her kids. She acts so tough, but when she's with them she's different, tender.

LYNN. You know she used to be a model?

ALISON. I didn't know that.

LYNN. Oh yeah. Not on runways or anything like that, but a lot of catalogs and hands sometimes. She traveled all over. She told me when she met Kevin, she was more than ready to give it up, but, between you and me, I think she misses it.

(to herself:)

Maybe that's her problem.

ALISON. AARON, STOP THAT! God, will you listen to me. I never loved anyone as much as I love my kids and yet I yell at them more and louder than I've ever yelled at anyone in my entire life. And I'm not a person who yells.

LYNN. Me neither. Never have been. WHAT? NO. ABSO-LUTELY NOT.

ALISON. Sometimes I think, who is that mean woman yelling at my children?

LYNN. Maybe it's because when we don't yell, nobody listens.

ALISON. Yeah, but I despise myself when I lose control like that. It scares me sometimes that I won't be able to find my way back.

(**LYNN** *looks at* **ALISON**, *sympathetically.*)

LYNN. Alison, look, maybe I can help you out someway… call me later…oh, that's no good, my mother-in-law's coming for dinner…what about tonight…oh, that's no good, I have calls to make for the zoo trip…can you call me tomorrow morning between 9 and 9:10?

(**NANCY** *enters.*)

NANCY. Listen to this: I told Gloria she was doing a great job letting them score and she gets mad and says 'Who's letting them?' Jane didn't tell her the plan.

(*The three women watch the game.*)

LYNN. They have gotten much better since the start of the season, haven't they? You know, I've never seen the boys looking so…intense. Look at them.

(*The three women continue watching.*)

ALISON. They do look pretty determined, don't they?

NANCY. I think they look…mean. Is that possible?

LYNN. Oh, no, they're only eight.

(*A whistle blows.*)

ALISON. Team B again? What's with that? HEY, THEY JUST PLAYED!

NANCY. So we don't play again until…?

LYNN. Until B finishes, then C and D play, and then us…

NANCY. Oh God.

(**NANCY** *sits down, depressed, staring at the field.*)

NANCY. B…C…D…A…my life is flashing before my eyes.

(**LYNN** *sits down next to* **NANCY**, *looks at her watch, then stares out in the same direction as* **NANCY**. **ALISON** *watches them for a moment, starts to speak then changes her mind and sits next to them. Resigned, they stare ahead blankly as the lights dim.*)

End of Scene Two

Scene Three

(As the lights come up, the women have not moved. They sit in the same positions, staring ahead.)

NANCY. I finished my life, now your life is flashing before my eyes.

ALISON. Oh no, Aaron's goalie. AARON! DON'T PUT YOUR HEAD THROUGH THE HOLES IN THE NET, YOU'LL GET STUCK!

LYNN. Hold everything. What's the ref doing? He's taking off...yes, ladies and gentlemen, he's removing his outer shirt, leaving a very tight black tee shirt...Judges, your scores please. Yes, a perfect ten for the man in the skin tight shirt...

ALISON. He gets hot easily.

NANCY. It's not that hot. I think he likes showing off. Who is he anyway?

LYNN. A new gym teacher at the high school.

ALISON. I've run into him jogging. His name is David.

LYNN. You jog?

ALISON. HEY! DAVID! OVER HERE, IT'S ALISON! NICE SHIRT!

NANCY. I'm sorry, but I don't get the shirt. Either that or I've truly lost the ability to look at another man with any interest whatsoever. The last time I looked that carefully at a man's shirt was when the gynecologist...

(ALISON and NANCY stare at her.)

NANCY. Never mind.

LYNN. Hey, Nancy, I'm serious, I have to know if you can do the Bronx Zoo.

NANCY. *(exasperated)* Can't you ask somebody else?

LYNN. There's no one left. You're the bottom of the barrel, you know what I mean, my last resort. What's with you?

NANCY. *(points to her head)* Must be my injury.

LYNN. I'm not talking about today. This has been going on for months. You don't even pick up the phone anymore.

NANCY. *(takes an aspirin)* Whatever it is, it's killing me.

LYNN. What's that suppose to mean, killing you?

NANCY. I don't know.

ALISON. DAVID! WHAT'S GOING ON? WHY ARE THEY STOPPING?

LYNN. YEAH, COME ON.

(NANCY takes out her camera again. LYNN reaches into her canvas bag and pulls out books, lists and envelopes.)

LYNN. Well then, soccer moms, while we're waiting...

NANCY. I hate that. It is so diminishing to be lumped into a group called soccer moms.

LYNN. *(sighs)* All right then, noble and intelligent women whose children play soccer every fucking weekend...

NANCY. *(laughs, shocked)* Lynn!

LYNN. *(looking around, surprised at herself)* Oh my God! I can't believe I said that. Geez, were there any kids around? I am really losing it. What I'm trying to say is we might as well be productive while we wait.

NANCY. Oh God. Please no.

ALISON. I don't mind helping.

LYNN. First, you take an envelope that says *The Happy Man and his Dump Truck* on the front, then you take a copy of the book...and put it in, like so....

(LYNN hands them to ALISON and NANCY.)

(NANCY looks at the envelopes.)

NANCY. Uh...Lynn, none of them say *Happy Man*, they're all *Good Night Moon*. Look.

(LYNN frantically starts looking through the envelopes.)

LYNN. Oh God, these are all wrong. No one ever takes this stuff seriously and then it's up to me to fix it.

(She massages her temples.)

I'm getting a headache the size of Mt. Vesuvius.

ALISON. Oh good, they're starting again.

NANCY. Wow, look at Linda Ackerman go. Uh oh, right through Aaron's legs into the net!

ALISON. Oh God, oh no, he's bending over. Is he crying?

NANCY/LYNN. IS HE HURT?

ALISON. Oh dear, I'll be right back.

*(**ALISON** exits.)*

LYNN. He's okay. I feel bad, it's so tough being the goalie. Now what? This is endless, they've stopped again.

NANCY. *(looking through the book)* I've always liked this book.

LYNN. Yeah, good story.

NANCY. Good characters. I like the man – his life is simple. He's happy. Rides around all day giving animals a lift. No demands, no pressures. And the pig – I like the pig.

LYNN. Oh yeah, me too. I like when they slide out of the truck after the ride.

NANCY. And the way the man is always singing…

(They look at one another, suddenly aware of the book they are discussing.)

We're drowning here, you know.

LYNN. What else is new?

*(**NANCY** picks up **ALISON**'s book.)*

NANCY. What's this? *Soccer for Dummies…* Geez, what's with her and soccer? And what's she mean, this is an 'important' day.

*(As she look through the book a paper falls out. **NANCY** picks it up and starts to put it back, but glances down at it.)*

LYNN. What's that?

NANCY. Looks like a joke…

LYNN. Go on, read it!

NANCY. *(looks around)* I don't want her to see me.

LYNN. Oh, come on, she's not looking. I can hear Aaron from here demanding to go home. Besides, nobody's budging. I need a laugh.

NANCY. All right. Here goes. A married couple checks into a hotel, but the room has two single beds so they each take one. After a while, the husband says, "Why don't you come over here for a little visit, my sugar plum," and she says, "All right," but on the way over she stubs her toe. "Oh no," the man says, "You poor thing, did you hurt your cute little toesie, wosies? Let me kiss that cute itty, bitty toe and make it all better. You come right over here." So over she goes and they make love and fall asleep. A little while later, the single bed is too crowded so the woman moves over toward her bed, but slips on the rug, once again stubbing her toe. "Ow," she cries to which the man growls, "Why don't you pick up your God damned feet?"

(NANCY turns the paper over, looking for more. They look at one another confused, laugh a little and shrug.)

LYNN. That's not a joke, that's life as we know it.

(NANCY and LYNN laugh. NANCY puts the joke away.)

NANCY. Wonder what it's for.

LYNN. *(looks at her watch)* They better hurry up. Lennie's mother is never late. In fact, she always arrives an hour early, hoping to catch me making a mistake. Sometimes I burn something just to make her happy.

NANCY. What'd Lennie say when you told him you didn't want her coming Saturday and Sunday?

LYNN. I didn't, I lost my nerve. Oh no, look, now Alison's son's running away from her. Wow, look at her go. She's in fantastic shape, isn't she?

NANCY. Yeah. Jack was five before I quit using his birth as an excuse for extra pounds. I'd say, oh, but I just had a baby…and then he'd come bounding into the room asking for the keys to the car.

(**ALISON** *enters.*)

ALISON. He's okay now. I told him that there were ten boys in front of him – if it gets to him, they all fouled up first. David says they're not going to start playing again for a while.

(**ALISON** *watches as* **LYNN** *works on the books and envelopes.*)

ALISON. I can't believe how much you do, Lynn.

NANCY. It's involuntary. Jane may have bottled up attorney aggression, but this one has a build up of nurturing from her days as a social worker.

ALISON. A social worker? I didn't know you were anything.

LYNN. Thanks a lot.

ALISON. I mean, what I mean is…that's not what I meant. I meant…

LYNN. It's all right, Alison, my mother used to say treat each day like one lifetime. Balance all the things in a day that you'd like to balance in your entire life.

NANCY. Wow. I have a hard time balancing dinner.

LYNN. Tell me about it, it's a tough act to follow.

NANCY. My mother used to read all the time.

LYNN. So, she read.

NANCY. I mean all the time. I don't think her life went the way she had hoped, so she lived other lives every time she opened a new book. She escaped.

ALISON. At least she was in the house. My mother left when I was thirteen.

LYNN. Oh Alison, that's so sad.

NANCY. That must have been rough.

ALISON. It was. But I had my dad and he was great. I loved him for trying to make it up to me…even though most of the time he didn't really know how.

LYNN. (*looks out at the field*) Makes you wonder what we're doing to them that they'll talk about some day on a soccer field.

NANCY. I'm sure it's stuff we have no idea we're doing.

(*pause*)

LYNN. Well, there's no getting around it, wherever you go, there's the three of you...you, your mother and your father. For better or worse.

(*looks at* ALISON)

Whether you knew them or not.

(*looks at the field*)

Look! Something's happening over there.

NANCY. Looks like the ref's leaving.

LYNN. Maybe it's his wife. She's due any minute – he's probably going to the hospital.

ALISON. What? He's not married.

LYNN. Realllly...well, married or not, she's ready to give birth!

(ALISON *hurriedly takes the joke out of the book.*)

ALISON. DAVID! WAIT A MINUTE!

(*She turns quickly to* LYNN, *speaking urgently and impatiently.*)

So, Lynn, can you take care of my kids or not?

LYNN. (*startled*) Uh...yeah, sure, I guess so.

(ALISON *exits.* LYNN *and* NANCY *watch her, then look at each other.*)

NANCY. Why is she giving the gym teacher a sexy joke?

LYNN. Oh, look, there's Alison's husband getting Adele out of the car. ALISON! HEY! YOUR HUSBAND'S HERE!

NANCY. I don't think she cares.

LYNN. (*fixing her hair and adjusting her shirt*) Oh great. There's Gloria taking our picture for that damn slide show at the awards ceremony. Say cheese.

(NANCY *immediately whirls around, out of habit, tilting her head and smiling radiantly.*)

NANCY. Never say anything. Your mouth will be open for the picture and you'll look terrible.

(*NANCY poses again, then* **NANCY** *and* **LYNN** *put their arms around each other and smile.*)

(**ALISON** *enters.* **LYNN** *and* **NANCY** *watch her with curiosity.*)

NANCY. So?

ALISON. What? Oh, yeah, his wife's in labor, no big deal. Let's just drop it.

NANCY. Drop what?

LYNN. Ron took your daughter. He pushed her to the other side of the field.

ALISON. (*angrily*) Yeah, sure he did. It'd never occur to him to come over and say 'Hi, how are you, how's the game?'

(*Frustrated, she walks to the sideline, yelling.*)

COME ON, WHAT ABOUT US, DAMN IT! TEAM D IS THROUGH, LOOK AT THEM! GET A BACK OUT THERE! Oh, look! He is! He's yelling for A!

LYNN. Wow, Jeremy Nolan just tackled his mother…GETTING A LITTLE ROUGH OUT THERE, ISN'T IT?

NANCY. IS SHE OKAY?…Is she moving?…Ah, there, she's back on her feet…

LYNN. Now remember, make it look good, but let them win.

NANCY. Yes, right, we have to go easy on them.

ALISON. (*puts out her hand*) Hey!

LYNN. What?

ALISON. You know, like they do, before they run out on the field.

(**NANCY** *stares at* **ALISON**'s *hand, rolls her eyes and walks off, exiting.* **LYNN** *and* **ALISON** *slap hands.* **LYNN** *grimces in pain, shaking her hand, then follows* **ALISON**, *exiting.*)

End of Scene Three

Scene Four

(The sound of a whistle. **LYNN** *enters and drops onto the bench.* **NANCY** *enters quickly, excited. They shed the outer layers of clothes. They're out of breath, but not quite as much as the first time they played.)*

NANCY. I feel muscles that have been dormant for eight years.

LYNN. What I wouldn't give for a cigarette.

NANCY. You don't smoke.

LYNN. *(caught)* Oh…right. I forgot.

NANCY. Forgot? Lynn, you smoke?

LYNN. Ssssh. When I'm stressed. And…I am getting…. very…stressed.

ALISON. I'm glad they took Aaron off the goal.

LYNN. Yeah, but now it's Gordon Grant and he's such a smart aleck. He's the one that kicked the ball at Nancy. You know how he smirks when he keeps it from going in? I never gave it much thought before, but when he smirked at me I felt like kicking the ball into his stomach.

ALISON. It was good of you to let them get that goal, Lynn.

LYNN. Oh…yeah…sure.

NANCY. Yeah, Lynn, you were very convincing. It looked like you were really trying to block it from going in.

LYNN. Well, that was our plan, right? Make it look good. And what about you, Nancy? I could have sworn you were aiming right for the goal when you kicked it. That was one powerful kick.

ALISON. Yeah, it's a good thing Aaron stopped it before it went in.

NANCY. …good thing…

LYNN. So, now what, it's one to one, right? We just let them get a few more and it's over.

ALISON. Yep. They win. Just like you wanted.

NANCY. Yeah. Right. I guess so.

    (pause)

    You know, it occurred to me out there. Maybe...

LYNN. Maybe what?

NANCY. Maybe we shouldn't make it too easy for them. We don't want them to get on to us.

ALISON. I was thinking the same thing. They'll start getting suspicious.

LYNN. What? I thought we didn't want them to feel bad... remember?

NANCY. Of course we don't want them to feel bad, I'm just not sure what kind of lesson it is for them if we let them win without some kind of fight.

ALISON. No one's going to let them win this easily when they get out into the real world.

LYNN. They're in the third grade!

NANCY. They have to learn sometime.

LYNN. I guess, but...

NANCY. We're doing it for them, Lynn.

LYNN. I guess it's not like they need a handicap.

NANCY. That's an understatement.

LYNN. In fact, is it my imagination or are they playing a little too rough?

ALISON. Maybe we should get more organized. Now, Nancy, next time, kick it to me and run down toward the goal and I'll get it back to you. And, listen, about Gordon... if you kick it to the right of him, you'll have a better chance. I watched him all season and he's no good on his right side.

NANCY. I've seen that too. The ones to his right side always go in. And you have to watch out for Jeremy Nolan. It's not just his mom he goes after – he's like a wild man.

ALISON. I'll stay close to him.

LYNN. This doesn't feel right.

NANCY. Look at it this way – see that group of kids over

there, your son included. Do you think they're saying, "c'mon, guys, we don't want our moms to feel bad, let's give them a break."

LYNN. It's possible.

NANCY. Yeah, right. All right, then, look over there. See the dads – imagine this is the dads playing the sons game... okay? Now, remember, it's in front of the whole town – everyone is watching and the dads have a meeting before the game...you think Bob says, come on guys, let's go easy on them so they're not disappointed.

(ALISON picks up her soccer book and flips through it.)

LYNN. I thought we wanted to make them happy. You stood right there and said...

NANCY. We do, but you're missing the point, the point is...

ALISON. *(interrupting)* Listen, my book says, "Teach your child that hard work and an honest effort are often more important than victory." We're not being honest. We're tricking them. Our own kids.

LYNN. We are?

NANCY. Sure. What else does your book say, Alison?

ALISON. Let's see, fun, self-discipline, personal growth, blah, blah, here...teaching ethics, values, respect. It's not ethical to fool them, is it?

NANCY. No, of course not. If we don't respect ourselves, how can they?

ALISON. *(reading from the book)* "As long as they have tried their hardest, played their best, they are all winners, no matter what the final score."

NANCY. I'm just saying let's make them work a little for their win, that's all.

(They turn their heads toward the field.)

NANCY. Now what? Coach Bob is calling you over, Lynn.

LYNN. I'll be right back.

(LYNN exits.)

NANCY. Alison, what were you saying out there about kicking? Something about the laces?

ALISON. When you want more control of the ball, you use
   the inside of your foot. Right here. Like when you're
   dribbling...

   (She demonstrates.)

   But when you want full power, you pull your foot back
   and kick the ball with this part of your foot where your
   laces are. Right there. Watch.

   *(**ALISON** demonstrates, then **NANCY** tries it. **LYNN**
   enters.)*

LYNN. He said we should quit. He said he's ready to call the
   paramedics to bring over stretchers.

NANCY. You mean just stop and go home?

LYNN. Well, there is one condition. He said his condition is
   that he gets the...

   *(**LYNN** puts her thumbs together and holds up her index
   fingers, forming a "W." **NANCY** and **ALISON** look at
   LYNN blankly.)*

NANCY. What's that?

LYNN. The win.

   (makes the sign)

   W?

ALISON. What is he, nuts? They win because we give up?
   Who does he think we are?

LYNN. He didn't say they, he said <u>he</u>, so <u>he'll</u> get the...

   *(**LYNN** makes the "W" sign again. They look at one
   another, taking this in and start to laugh.)*

NANCY. I think when he said what about this...

   (makes the "W" sign)

   You should have said what about this...

   *(She puts up her two middle fingers. They laugh harder.
   ALISON hears something and walks toward the field.)*

ALISON. Jeremy Nolan's yelling something to Lynn.

(She walks toward the field.)

He wants to make sure that Lynn keeps playing – he says it'll help them rack up a lot of points.

LYNN. WHAT? OH, YOU THINK SO, YOU LITTLE…I am so tired of being the one who…ah, forget it. This day is really starting to get on my nerves.

(She turns and trips over the bag of books.)

And so is the happy man and his damn truck.

*(**LYNN** picks up all her bags and drops them behind the bench. **NANCY** looks toward the field.)*

NANCY. This has gone from absurd to downright annoying.

ALISON. Oh no, Aaron's stuck in the net again, I'll be right back.

*(**ALISON** exits.)*

NANCY. I'm running this thing next year.

LYNN. You? Don't make me laugh. The day you run something, I'll run up a flag.

NANCY. Well, I may not be 'Blimpie Lunch Mom', but I help sometimes.

LYNN. Oh sure, you can't even give me a straight answer about the Bronx Zoo.

NANCY. You're not serious.

LYNN. I ask and you say no. You weren't at the auction, you didn't help hang the art show, you weren't at…

NANCY. What about the Halloween parade?

LYNN. You watched. That was very helpful.

*(**NANCY** picks up her camera and walks away from **LYNN**, adjusting her lens.)*

NANCY. What's with you? That's not fair.

LYNN. Fair? I wind up doing everything for everyone every day of the week and I'm not fair? I am tired of being the one who is so understanding of everyone – that's what I'm tired of. There's always some excuse with you.

NANCY. You mean like I'd rather be with my own children?

LYNN. Oh and I don't? What we do is for all the kids.

NANCY. We? You mean the elite grand order of mothers in charge.

LYNN. Somebody has to. Forget it. I didn't mean to make it into a big thing.

NANCY. It's too late, you made it into a big thing. What about helping out at the nurse's office? What about that?

LYNN. You did it once. Congratulations.

NANCY. Well, maybe if you were home more, your kids wouldn't be wandering around so...

LYNN. So what? Go on. Going on a class trip doesn't mean you've sold your soul to the devil, you know.

NANCY. Maybe not to you.

LYNN. Why do you think you're dealing with anything more than the rest of us? Yeah, it's lonely and isolated, but it might be a heck of a lot easier if you joined in.

NANCY. I don't understand why everyone thinks becoming a mother means you become a different person. When I was a kid I could never just walk onto a playground and start talking with the other kids. It took me forever. Now I'm suppose to walk onto a playground, waving and smiling like Miss Extrovert, joining right in with all the chitchat. It's very hard for me. And, believe me, I know this is totally irrelevant to anything, but I am trying to make some progress with my work.

LYNN. What work?

NANCY. My...you know...photography.

LYNN. Don't take this the wrong way, Nancy, but I swear to God, I have never seen one picture you've taken, not one.

(**NANCY** *looks at* **LYNN** *about to answer, but decides against it.*)

NANCY. Look, I'm just not interested in class trips or trips of any kind, okay? If you want to knock yourself out with that "stuff," great, do it, but, please, leave me out of it.

LYNN. I knock myself out with that "stuff" because I'm doing something good for the kids, and you know what really gets me? Not the work, not the kids, but having other parents look down their nose at me like I'm some no-brain volunteer who's not smart enough to be doing something else. I choose to do this – I left a great job, a great job! And you know why? Because I like having my kids light up like the Fourth of July when they see me in the school. And I like to be there at that unpredictable moment when one of their most private thoughts is presented to me like a gift. It's what I want to do and I wouldn't trade it for anything.

NANCY. You got it wrong, Lynn, nobody looks down at you. They're intimidated by you. But they admire you. I admire you, don't you know that? It's just...

(She sighs.)

You know why you don't see any pictures?

(NANCY *turns her bag over and rolls of undeveloped film fall out.)*

NANCY. I never develop them.

LYNN. Why not?

NANCY. I say it's the kids' fault. That I don't have time. I guess that's partially true, but...it's more than that... there's something else...

LYNN. What? Is it what you said before, about killing you. What's killing you?

NANCY. I keep thinking I'm missing out on something. I used to have this ecstasy about life that would make me feel so alive. And now...

LYNN. Now what Nancy? What?

NANCY. Oh Lynn. In the past six months, there was both Mary and my sister-in-law. Did you know that right here, on this bench, Mary sat next to me one Sunday afternoon just a year ago. It was a game that very few of us showed up for – she looked around, searching for people, and then she said, with such anger in her voice that she was shaking, "Where is everybody? What could they be doing that's so much more important than watching their children play?" I was allowed for a few moments to look through the eyes of a woman who was seeing life as clearly as you can see it – with a pure and unobstructed vision. And her words hit me. Profoundly. Where was everybody? She knew that with what time she had left all she wanted to do was look at her children.

LYNN. That was Mary.

NANCY. And then, not more than a couple of months after that, my sister-in-law made that rare visit to our house. I told you about her – she had breast cancer.

LYNN. Joanne, right?

NANCY. Yeah, Joanne. She said to me, how are you and I started talking about the kids and she said, no, no, you, how are you, are you going back to work, are you really going to become a photographer, and before I could answer she begins to cry and says she wished she had worked at something that was just hers, that belonged to her. That she had actually written the book that she always talked about, but never took the time to do. She had two wonderful boys, but this is what she wanted to talk about. So, you see – children, work, there's always going to be some regret, so I keep thinking if I could just find out what mine will be, maybe I could do something about it. Whatever it is, I think if I don't do something soon, it's going to be too late. The only thing I know for sure is…my kids…they mean everything to me, so, see? What am I talking about?

LYNN. Maybe…

(shrugs and puts her arm around **NANCY***)*

Who wakes up thinking they're going to get hit in the head with a soccer ball?

NANCY. Right.

(They smile and pick up the rolls of film. **ALISON** *enters, excited, rubbing her hands together, watching the field.)*

ALISON. Haven't you been watching?

LYNN. What? No. I didn't realize they started again.

ALISON. I think you two better shut up and look at what's going on. We look like idiots out there. Everyone's laughing at us. No, it's worse than that. They're feeling sorry for us.

NANCY. They feel sorry for us?

ALISON. Some guy said, let's just end this and put them out of their misery.

NANCY. What, they want to shoot us?

LYNN. What's happening to everyone today? It's just a game.

NANCY. It's our own fault. We could go for it, but we stop ourselves. We're our own oppressors.

LYNN. Are you talking about the game?

ALISON. They're getting ready over there. You're absolutely right, Nancy. Are we just going to keep standing there while they walk all over us?

NANCY. What did you say you want me to do? I pass it to you and...

ALISON. ...You pass it to me and run like hell for the goal, I'll be looking for you, and then I'll get it back to you and you shoot.

NANCY. If we catch them off guard, we'll have a better chance. HEY, BOB!

(holds up the "W" sign with her fingers)

FORGET IT! WE'RE STILL IN THIS GAME!

(The whistle blows.)

ALISON. All right then. We're up again. If we're going to play, let's play.

(ALISON pulls off her long pants and sweat shirt. Underneath, she has short jogging pants and a tee shirt on. She opens her duffel bag, takes out a clip and puts her hair up, then puts sweat bands on around her wrists. She puts on sun glasses. LYNN and NANCY stare at her.)

ALISON. Look, I was voted best athlete in high school. I ran cross country, was captain of the basketball team and won state trophies for both. But Ron hated me playing sports, thought it made me too aggressive. So I gave it up. But, today, today I came prepared to play and then you guys say, "Let's give it to them," so wanting you to like me, to be one of the gang, I say, okay, but... enough is enough...how many goals do we need to make it look good?

LYNN. As many as we can. I mean, right?

NANCY. Absolutely.

ALISON. Okay, let's do it.

(This time the slapping of hands is coordinated and sure. They laugh and run off quickly.)

End of Scene Four

Scene Five

(In the blackout we hear **LYNN***,* **NANCY** *and* **ALISON** *offstage:)*

LYNN. *(offstage)* Alison, over here.

ALISON. *(offstage)* Lynn, go around that kid.

(Sound of a whistle.)

NANCY. *(offstage)* He fouled, I didn't.

LYNN. *(offstage)* LOOK OUT!

(There is the sound of an eight year old crying loudly. Lights come up as **ALISON***,* **LYNN** *and* **NANCY** *run back to the bench.)*

NANCY. I didn't even see him.

LYNN. It's not your fault. He's so small.

NANCY. I know, but I just ran him down. You think he's all right?

ALISON. I can't tell. Everybody's standing around him.

NANCY. You think I should go over there?

LYNN. I wouldn't. Did you see the way his mother glared at you? I saw her clench her fist.

NANCY. It was an accident.

LYNN. Tell her. I'd give her some time to cool off if I were you. Besides, you know him, he cries if you look at him funny.

NANCY. *(waving toward the field)* SORRY!

LYNN. You think they won't count our goal because he got hurt?

NANCY. What? What's one thing go to do with the other?

LYNN. They might say you fouled him.

NANCY. I didn't foul him! I got that goal fair and square.

ALISON. They won't take away our goal, but he'll get a direct free kick for that other thing you did.

NANCY. God, he practically jumps on you and then everybody looks at you like you're some kind of bully. Of course, I really didn't mean to kick him.

LYNN. Of course you didn't.

ALISON. This is the best I've ever seen them play.

(They turn toward the field.)

NANCY. What'd that kid just say to us? Him. Right there.

LYNN. He said, "You guys stink."

NANCY. We stink? COME OVER HERE. WHAT KIND OF SPORTSMANSHIP IS THAT?...Oh sure, HE RUNS OFF...BIG TALKER!

ALISON. We definitely have to strategize a little better. What is Jane's problem? She started out so strong and now...

LYNN. I think she's out of wind.

NANCY. Yeah, well so am I.

ALISON. And what's Gloria's story? She should never have been goalie.

LYNN. Would have made all the difference if we had someone there who knew what she was doing.

NANCY. You think she let him get it in because it was her kid?

LYNN. I don't think so. She said 'shit' like she meant it.

(They gulp down their water, wiping their foreheads with their arms. A whistle blows.)

LYNN. WHAT?...Good. Half-time, we can regroup. It's so hard once they surround you. It's like being in the middle of a mob.

NANCY. A mob of little people. Little feet, little hands, little voices. I felt like kicking them away from me.

LYNN. So you did kick him on purpose.

NANCY. GLORIA, HOW IS HE? IS HE OKAY?

ALISON. We were better this time around, don't you think?

NANCY. Oh definitely. I think Bob's getting nervous. He keeps huddling with the boys.

ALISON. I think we need more unity in the second half. I have an idea.

NANCY. What?

ALISON. Let's take the best players from all the teams and put them together.

(**LYNN** and **NANCY** perk up, interested.)

LYNN. Like an all-star team!

ALISON. Yeah. I mean, Jane may be a little winded but she really knows how to get it into the net.

NANCY. Lynn, you talk to her. See what she says.

LYNN. If she says yes, who do we want?

ALISON. Jane, Gloria, but only if she's not goalie, group D.

NANCY. Forget D. They left for drinks ten minutes ago.

ALISON. We don't need them. Then that group over there from B and C. And us.

LYNN. The three of us?

ALISON. Of course. Right, Nancy?

NANCY. Of course the three of us. What? You think maybe not me?

ALISON. No, I thought she was talking about me.

LYNN. I was talking about me.

NANCY. I think we need a little more self-confidence if we're going to win this game.

LYNN. Win?

NANCY. I didn't say win, I said play better. Go on, Lynn, see what she says. And ask her if Alison can be our coach.

ALISON. Me?

NANCY. We need someone who can say 'direct free kick' and know what it means. Lynn, someone's yelling your name. There, that woman with the…what the hell is that, a bulldog? You know how they say people and their pets start to look alike? Take a look at…

LYNN. Perfect. It's my mother-in-law. HI…DID YOU COME TO WATCH ME PLAY?…'Of course not,' she says. That figures…WHAT?…WHAT AM I MAKING FOR DINNER? WELL, I'LL TELL YOU…RESERVATIONS! THAT'S WHAT I'M MAKING FOR DINNER…RESER-VATIONS TO A RESTAURANT…AND WE'RE NOT

GOING UNTIL I'M FINISHED HERE…SO WHY
DON'T YOU GO SIT SOMEWHERE AND WATCH?…
LARRY, YOUR GRANDMOTHER'S HERE! No sur-
prise who she's rooting for.

ALISON. Your son?

LYNN. My husband.

ALISON. But he's not playing.

LYNN. He's not running for President either, but that didn't
stop her from writing him in. JANE!

(**LYNN** *exits.*)

ALISON. Thanks for the coach thing. I hope I do it right.

NANCY. You'll be fine.

ALISON. Nancy, I know that you don't like to talk…

NANCY. Alison. It's not that I don't like to talk. It's just that
I have a hard time focusing. Like now, please, don't
get insulted if I keep staring at that tree, but Jack is
getting higher and higher and I may have to bolt over
there and throw myself under him when he falls. Isn't
that your husband yelling?

(**ALISON** *walks toward the parking lot.*)

ALISON. RON, WHAT?…BUT IT'S ALMOST OVER…I
CAN'T…I'M SORRY. I DIDN'T KNOW IT WAS GOING
TO TAKE SO LONG…OKAY, OKAY…FINE…

(*Embarrassed, she looks at* **NANCY**, *but* **NANCY** *watches
the tree, pretending not to hear.*)

RON! SSSSSHHHHHH. CALM DOWN. JUST KEEP
THE STROLLER MOVING, SHE'S HAPPIER WHEN
SHE'S MOVING. OKAY, FINE.

He wants to go home and take a nap.

NANCY. Hmmmmm.

ALISON. He wants me to leave. He's taking Adele for a walk,
then he said we're leaving…whether it's over or not…

NANCY. You shouldn't let him yell at you like that.

ALISON. He's tired.

NANCY. That has nothing to do with it.

ALISON. I feel like I'm going...nuts...Ron works all the time...nights...weekends...and...

(ALISON stops talking.)

NANCY. And?

ALISON. There's someone else.

(NANCY stops watching the tree and stares at ALISON.)

NANCY. Oh Alison, I heard. No! What I mean is, I'm so sorry. When did you find out?...WHAT? FINE. I DON'T CARE. CLIMB HIGHER. DON'T WORRY SO MUCH...Go on, Alison. How did you find out? Did you catch them together?

ALISON. Not him. Me.

NANCY. You?

ALISON. I know. It's unbelievable. I haven't told one person.

NANCY. *(quickly)* Well, then, tell me.

(catching herself)

I mean, you can tell me.

(LYNN enters.)

LYNN. It's all set. After C plays, then it's all-stars. Jane was a little too excited by the whole thing, but I'm sure she'll calm down. And Alison's the coach.

(NANCY and ALISON look at LYNN blankly.)

LYNN. What's the matter? Are you talking about me?

NANCY. Better than that.

LYNN. Well, don't let me interrupt.

ALISON. It's not like I actually cheated on him...

LYNN. What?

(turns on NANCY)

And you have me over there talking about soccer?

ALISON. It's not like I was looking for it. It's just that things at home...I mean, Ron and I were so young when we got married – it was like we were two single people in a

house with a baby. I went right from my father to Ron.
I haven't been alone a day in my life. And then when
the second one came along…I'm in so over my head.
And then Ron decides we should move here. He has
three ways of dealing with problems – move, work or
travel. Anything, but sit down and talk.

NANCY. When I say I want to talk, Kevin holds up his fingers like this, like a cross holding off a vampire, "no,
please, no."

ALISON. It's like I thought we both signed on for this ride,
but he's checked out. Like I'm a single parent and I
don't know what I'm doing.

NANCY. So who does?

ALISON. All of you.

(gestures toward the field)

Everybody.

LYNN. Oh come on, Alison, nobody knows if they're doing
it right. That's what's so insane about this job – the
results are all over the place. You make progress one
week and slide back the next. We all pray they turn out
happy, but who knows?

NANCY. So who is it?

LYNN. Do we know him?

NANCY. Are you going to run away together?

LYNN. Is he married?

NANCY. Does he live in town?

LYNN. What about your children?

ALISON. It doesn't matter! I just found out it was all in my
mind anyhow. I came here today ready to turn my
whole life upside down and now I find out that that
wasn't even an option.

NANCY. You just found out? Oh my God. The gym teacher.

LYNN. The gym teacher?

ALISON. Yes.

NANCY. But he's on his way to…

ALISON. I know! Now. He never mentioned it.

NANCY. He never mentioned he had a wife who was about to have a baby?

ALISON. We wound up running every morning at the same time on the same road and we ran so well together that we actually planned our meetings. Now that I think back all these months, I'm the one who's been doing all the talking.

LYNN. You can run and talk at the same time?

ALISON. I thought he was looking at me in that way that means he wanted to, you know, get serious...but I guess it was just that crazed runner look...he was such a good listener.

LYNN. Maybe he was just out of breath and couldn't talk.

ALISON. See, that's why I was going away next week. To a place at the beach where I could be alone and think about what to do about my life. I was going to ask him if he'd like to visit me there – to talk – to see if he might be someone who could help me or be interested in a woman with two kids.

LYNN. Wow. But what about the joke? Why did you give that to him?

NANCY. *(caught)* What joke?

ALISON. You read my joke?

(LYNN and NANCY exchange guilty looks.)

LYNN. Yes. Yes, we read your joke. It fell out of your book and we needed a laugh.

ALISON. Who doesn't? David, he loves jokes. But I'm lousy at remembering them so I wrote it down. Ron's so stressed out all the time. It's like he's too tired to laugh. Oh God. Sometimes at night I lie in bed next to Ron wondering how did I ever wind up like this...

NANCY. Look, Alison, I'm no therapist and I've got a kid in a tree...

LYNN. Not anymore, he just fell out.

(Without missing a beat, NANCY exits, running.

ALISON *and* **LYNN** *stand frozen, watching.)*

ALISON. Look, he's laughing. I think he's okay.

LYNN. God, every fiber of your being focused on every fiber of their being. It's exhausting.

*(***NANCY*** enters, shaking her head.)*

NANCY. God, my heart stopped.

LYNN. Mine too.

NANCY. I can't believe it, he said it was fun. Like flying.

(They all sigh, relieved.)

NANCY. *(continuing; looks toward Jack, concerned)* He looks okay, doesn't he?

LYNN. Sure. Don't worry.

NANCY. Oh. Look, he's chasing Sally. He's definitely okay.

LYNN. So…where were we? I…uh…oh yeah, you were saying you're no therapist…

NANCY. Oh yeah, it seems to me Alison's waiting for Ron to make the move and it has to be her. Not Ron, not David. See, it's not that the gym teacher fantasy is wrong, but it's just a fantasy…

LYNN. Right! I mean, hey, gym teacher, auto mechanic, the dry cleaner…

NANCY. The dry cleaner?

LYNN. *(shrugs)* Leave me alone…

NANCY. Alison, it's up to you to make it better. You make it part of the deal that you have to be listened to. If nobody asks them to change, why should they?

ALISON. Before she left my mother used to say, you marry who you marry and don't try changing him cause it ain't gonna happen.

LYNN. Why does it have to be called changing – didn't anyone ever hear of maturing? Look, Lennie's a wonderful man, I'm crazy about him and would never say a word against him…*but*…sometimes he is not a great listener – he says so himself. Just last month my back went out so badly I could hardly move, let alone, have...well, you know.

NANCY. Sex?

LYNN. Right. So Lennie sees the shape I'm in and I assume understands what's going on. I apologize and everything. "Sorry, Len," I said, "but what can I do? I'm in pain." So there's no contact for about a week and he is not a happy camper –

NANCY. After a week?

LYNN. Yeah. And so he comes to me with this look of distress on his face. He says he knows I'm in pain, but would I consider a deal.

NANCY. One week and he's upset? He thinks that's a long time?

LYNN. Isn't it?

ALISON. Not in my house.

NANCY. Not in my house. You're okay with once a week?

LYNN. I didn't say once a week.

NANCY. Couldn't imagine. So what – every other?

LYNN. Two or three times a week.

NANCY. Two or three times – a week?

ALISON. I have friends who go a month.

LYNN. You're kidding.

NANCY. I have friends who go many months.

LYNN. God, I'd be nuts.

NANCY. You would?

LYNN. Certifiable. Lock me up.

NANCY. This is a whole new side to you, Lynn.

LYNN. Well, it's not the kind of information I include on the P.T.A. agenda. Why, how often do you and Kevin...?

NANCY. Not two or three times a week.

ALISON. Even when Ron's home, he's not really interested.

LYNN. Geez, no wonder you're looking at the gym teacher. Now there I would draw the line. I would get seriously cranky.

NANCY. You are a very interesting woman.

LYNN. Can I finish?

NANCY. By all means. So what was Lennie's deal?

LYNN. That if I have sex with him he would sit down with me for forty five minutes and listen to every single thing I said and, not only that, he would try to respond in some kind of coherent and intelligent way to every issue I brought up instead of staring at me with this dead, blank look in his eyes.

NANCY. What did you say?

LYNN. I said fine as long as we talk first, or else no deal. He wouldn't agree to that, of course, but he did throw in an extra fifteen minutes of talking…'for good behavior.'

(They laugh then they sit quietly for a moment. NANCY *looks toward the field.)*

NANCY. There goes team C. We're up next.

ALISON. You won't say anything about this to anyone, will you? About David?

*(*LYNN *and* NANCY *look at one another, unsure)*

Oh, come on, you have to think about it?

LYNN. Fine.

NANCY. Anyway, it's not like you slept with him.

(pause)

Right?

LYNN. Yeah, it was just in your head. It's not like you did anything.

NANCY. Right, Alison? Alison, yoo hoo…

ALISON. Look, maybe I got the wrong idea, but I'm not stupid.

LYNN. So, what are you saying? He gave you a…sign of some sort?

ALISON. Yeah, a 'sign,' that's right. What does it matter?

(She sighs and gestures toward the field.)

It seems like we're all in the same boat so you'd think there'd be this great sense of camaraderie or community or something. I don't feel like I'm a part of anything. If only I didn't feel so alone.

NANCY. But that's how we all feel. We all feel that no one understands our particular…thing. Lynn feels nobody appreciates or cares how much she does for the kids. She thinks they don't even know, but what she doesn't know is that husbands and wives huddle late at night and whisper to each other, "Thank God for Lynn. Thank God she does it."

LYNN. They do?

NANCY. Of course they do. Kevin and I do.

LYNN. *(to herself)* Really.

ALISON. I love my children so much…

(Her voice catches.)

…I used to love Ron. Who knows, maybe I still love him, but I'm so numb with frustration I don't know anymore. How can you be trapped by what you love? I look at them and cry because I love them so much and then I keep crying because…

(ALISON sits and puts her head in her hands and cries. NANCY and LYNN look helplessly at one another, each motioning for the other one to comfort ALISON.)

LYNN. Alison.

(ALISON doesn't look up. LYNN motions for NANCY to help.)

NANCY. Alison.

(pause)

Earlier today, what you were saying about losing your self, your old self…remember? It made me think of something. St. Martin? A trip I took with Kevin – to St. Martin.

(ALISON looks up. LYNN looks at NANCY curiously.)

What happened was his company sent some high com-
mission guys there – as a bonus. I wasn't eager to leave
the kids, but Kevin really wanted me to so I sent the
kids to my mother and off we go for one weekend.
Not even a long weekend. Arrive Friday night, leave
Sunday. The group's okay, some I like, some I don't,
it doesn't matter. I figure, "go, relax." So we get to this
wonderful hotel and first thing next morning we all
head for the beach, we have our chairs, our books, our
magazines, our sun block, our sunglasses and sun hats,
our radios, our food, our drink, everything we could
possibly need and sit in a semi-circle looking out at
this incredible water – blue, green, clear – too good
to be true. And we're all so happy talking about how
beautiful it is. And then, slowly, the kids creep in, okay,
fine, then, the houses, the towns, then the taxes, then
the school systems and then when we start comparing
which sports each town offers every summer I jump
out of my chair…a little too quickly. They all stop talking and stare up at me. I don't want to seem rude so I
say, "Anyone want to go for a walk?" and thank God no
one did. The exhaustion, the weariness just hung on
their faces like their eyes and noses and mouths – like
it was part of them – like they were born with it. And I
recognized that look. It's what I look at every morning
in the mirror.

(pause)

So I start walking. Walking and walking and walking.
Faster and faster. Feeling so good to be away from those
subjects. And then halfway down the beach I get to a lot
of rocks and coral blocking my way. No more sand. So
now I can either climb the rocks or go back. I decide to
take on the rocks. It's hard – I'm barefoot and can't get
my balance. I'm just about to fall face down on to these
sharp, jagged edges when my body suddenly springs
forward and I am filled with a memory.

(pause)

When I was growing up, our house was so far away from any others that there was never anyone around to play with. So, I would go off into the woods behind my house and play alone. I had this game of running on rocks. I would run as fast as I could, landing on the flat, stable ones because if my foot touched a loose one, I'd lose control and fall. There wasn't time to think, just move. So here I was, flying across these rocks and I'm ten again. So sure of myself. And when I got across the rocks, I was on a beach more beautiful than the one I was just on. But something was different. There weren't any beachbags or books or radios or chairs, just blankets and naked people stretched out speaking french.

LYNN. *(slightly surprised, softly)* Naked.

NANCY. One couple, thin, tan, naked, was sleeping on their backs. And their naked baby was lying across the mother's stomach with his head on her breast. It was like a beautiful painting. Others were talking quietly, but then I heard laughter. The kind of laughter that sounds like someone is saying "I love life" – and I turn and see two women in the water, coaxing a dog to come in, but she wouldn't. She kept running back and forth on the sand as they laughed and called to her. And I thought I want to be those women. I want to be naked in the water, laughing and speaking French.

LYNN. Were they lesbians?

NANCY. If they were lesbians, I wanted to be lesbians and if they weren't I didn't want to be. I wanted to be whatever they were. And, then, of course, I couldn't just stand there and stare so I kept walking. And I got to more rocks, harder and higher than the first. I climbed higher and higher until I got to the highest one. I stopped and looked out at this magnificent water and perfect sky and thought…one thing…one word…

ALISON. What?

LYNN. Freedom?

NANCY. Perspective. I had lost my perspective on life and by losing that I lost my spirit. I don't want to go anywhere or leave anyone. I love them. But I want it back...I want her back.

ALISON. Yes. Me too. That's what I want. How I felt when I was young, playing ball, running the bases. I was on a team, but I felt free.

NANCY. And when I ran in college. Nobody could get near me. Not even close. Nothing was missing then. You see, I had it...

(She clenches her fist.)

I had it, but I've lost it.

LYNN. *(softly, not surprised, but impressed)* You ran?

NANCY. Yeah.

(pause, proudly)

I ran.

ALISON. Then what? On the rocks.

NANCY. Then out of nowhere two black dogs start coming toward me. I figure this might be a good time to start back. So I start walking, trying to be very still as I walk, but they keep circling me, growling and barking. And I'm thinking to myself, well, this is just perfect, the watch dogs of the good life are growling, "who do you think you are? Get back to your chair and tell them you heard that strep throat was going around." It'd be nice if I could stand on those rocks every day, but I can't. It's not possible with the choices I've made. My choices. So I have to look somewhere else.

ALISON. But where?

NANCY. Look to yourself, Alison, you know what you want.

(After a long pause, ALISON turns her head toward the field. She speaks quietly.)

ALISON. Your husband's calling.

NANCY. *(far away, still on the beach)* What? Oh. Yeah. HI.

KEVIN, CHECK ON JACK, WILL YOU? HE FELL OUT OF A TREE, BUT HE'S FINE. THANK YOU!

(Pause. Lost in their own thoughts.)

ALISON. Lynn.

LYNN. Yeah.

ALISON. I'll go to the Bronx Zoo with you. Maybe if we had time, we could, you know, ride that skyride…the thing that flies high up over the zoo…maybe try to get some…you know…

LYNN. Perspective?

ALISON. Yeah.

LYNN. Thank you. I need all the help I can get.

NANCY. Oh, all right, I'll go. I'll go with you.

LYNN. There's just one thing, Alison, will you sit in the back of the bus with the third grade boys?

ALISON. What is that, some kind of initiation rite?

LYNN. Sort of.

ALISON. All right, fine.

NANCY. So we'll all go. Maybe, God forbid, we'll even have some fun.

(The whistle blows.)

ALISON. It's almost time. We ready?

NANCY. Oh yeah.

LYNN. What's our plan?

ALISON. First of all, Lynn, it's not necessary to stop to apologize when you take the ball away from them.

NANCY. Yeah, Lynn.

LYNN. We have to go with our strengths. Alison's strength is running and ours…is not.

ALISON. Your strength, Nancy, is kicking it in. And Lynn, I think you should be the goalie.

LYNN. Me?

ALISON. Yeah, before, when you were playing near our goal,

you were great, a natural. You know what they say…a
goalkeeper must have a good pair of hands.

NANCY. And from what we've heard here today, I would say
you're probably over-qualified.

ALISON. You'll be great. Nobody else could be as good as
you.

LYNN. That's true. All right, I'll do it.

NANCY. You know, Lynn, there's no law that says you can't
use your head.

LYNN. Well, that's an insulting thing to say. It's hard to
think with them all over you.

ALISON. No, literally, use your head. There's a spot, the flat
part of your forehead that's just below your hairline.
That's where you want it to hit. Now, goalies don't usu-
ally use their heads, but I say we go for it any way we
can, okay?

LYNN. You want me to bounce a soccer ball off my head, is
that what you're saying?

ALISON. And be aggressive. Don't let the ball hit you, you
hit it. That way you can control where it goes. You control it.

LYNN. Oh, Alison, look.

(**LYNN** *points.* **ALISON** *pauses.*)

ALISON. (*She speaks defiantly.*) RON! WHAT?…NO. I'M
NOT LEAVING!…THAT'S RIGHT! NOT UNTIL
THE GAME'S OVER. AND THEN I WANT US TO
HAVE DINNER ALONE, WITHOUT THE KIDS,
SO WE CAN TALK…TONIGHT I WANT TO TALK.
WHAT?…PIZZA?…FINE…WAIT, NO, Thai. I WANT
THAI FOOD. Okay, we ready?

NANCY. SALLY! SALLY, HONEY, WATCH MOMMY PLAY!
WATCH MOMMY!

LYNN. HEY, LENNIE! GET THE GIRLS! TELL THEM TO
WATCH THEIR MOTHER!

(*They put their hands on top of one another, very profes-
sionally, and yell, "GO."*)

(As the lights dim, the women move to three different areas, each in their own original spotlight from the prologue. The three women get into game positions. LYNN stands crouched as if in front of a goal, prepared to block any incoming balls.)

(ALISON and NANCY bend over with their hands on their knees in anticipation. A real soccer ball is not used during the game.)

(As the three women talk and mime their actions, they look ahead and not at one another.)

(No music is necessary, but, if used, something similar to Aaron Copland's Rodeo *is more appropriate than a traditional sports song.)*

ALISON. ALL RIGHT! STAY FOCUSED!

(LYNN moves quickly, stopping the ball with her foot, then throwing it away from her. She bends over to fix her sock.)

ALISON. LYNN! LOOK OUT!

(LYNN looks up too late. The ball goes through her legs for a goal. She bends over and looks through her legs after the ball.)

LYNN. Damn it! I'm sorry. Damn, now it's…I've lost track of the score.

ALISON. It's tied.

(LYNN groans.)

Don't let it throw you. Keep your eye on the ball.

(A gracefully choreographed 'soccer dance' begins. The three women kick, jump and spin – their bodies moving quickly and purposefully.)

ALISON. Nancy, stay back! Play defense.

NANCY. Defense? I spit on defense.

ALISON. Come on! I need you to back me up.

NANCY. Oh, fine.

(The action begins again. The ball comes to ALISON.

She stops it with her chest. It drops to the top of her knee, then to her foot as she kicks it. She waits, focused, then makes a lunging jump into the air.)

ALISON. Yeeeeooooo!

*(**ALISON** kicks the ball very hard down the field.)*

NANCY. Alison, nice kick!

*(**LYNN** prepares herself for the incoming ball.)*

ALISON. Look out! Here they come!

LYNN. *(to herself)* Here they come, here they come…get ready, Lynn.

*(With all her might, **LYNN** tilts her head forward and bounces the ball off the front of her head, driving it away from the goal.)*

LYNN. I did it! I did it! Did you see that?

ALISON. Nancy! Ready? Here it comes!

*(**NANCY** stops it with the inside of her thighs and then kicks it.)*

NANCY. Darn.

ALISON. Good try, Nancy. Okay, keep alert, here they come. If they get this one in, it's all over.

LYNN. Oh my God.

*(**LYNN** makes a long dive for the ball and rolls to a stop. She holds the ball up with one hand.)*

LYNN. I got it!

*(**NANCY** and **ALISON** cheer. **LYNN** throws the ball. The ball comes back to **ALISON**.)*

ALISON. This is our last chance. But don't worry about it, that's the trick – don't worry about the game, just play it.

NANCY. Alison, give it to me.

ALISON. What?

NANCY. Give it to me.

*(**ALISON** kicks the ball to her.)*

ALISON. It's all yours.

(**NANCY** *stops the ball and weaves from side to side, outmaneuvering everyone. She is sure of herself and in control of the ball.* **LYNN** *laughs and cheers.* **ALISON**'*s hands are high, in fists, watching.*)

LYNN. GO, NANCY, GO! RUN!

(*louder*)

SHOOT! SHOOOOOOOOOOOT!

(**NANCY** *kicks as hard as she can with the top of her foot and watches. They all stand, frozen, focused. As* **LYNN** *screams, throwing her arms in the air for victory, the lights come up on all of them.* **NANCY** *and* **ALISON** *run to* **LYNN**. *They hug, jump up and down screaming, then dance around one another.*)

ALISON. We did it, we did it! We won!

NANCY/LYNN. We won! We won!

(*They calm down, leaning on one another, breathing heavily, laughing and smiling. Suddenly, the realization of their win sets in and they become apprehensive, worried.*)

NANCY. (*looking around*) We won.

LYNN. And…they lost.

NANCY. Oh God, what did we just do?

LYNN. LARRY! HOW'RE YOU DOING, SWEETIE?

NANCY. JACK, YOU OKAY? I'M SORRY, I COULDN'T HEAR, WHAT DID YOU SAY?

ALISON. He said, "Way to go, Mom."

NANCY. Way to go?

(*pause*)

They don't look upset.

LYNN. They're not. Larry just said, "Yo, dude, did you see my mom do the head thing?"

(*pause*)

NANCY. It never occurred to me.

LYNN. I don't think it occurred to them either.

(They look at one another and smile. In high spirits, they walk to the bench to gather their belongings.)

ALISON. Lynn, that save you made – it was unbelievable.

NANCY. And your head, you used your head! That was very impressive. And your passes were perfect, Alison, they came right to me.

ALISON. It all came back – when to stay with it, when to pass it. It's all in the timing. But, Nancy, what about that goal?

LYNN. Yeah, Nancy, what about that?

NANCY. *(smiles at* **ALISON***)* Full power. Used the laces.

ALISON. Yeah, but there must have been ten kids in front of you.

LYNN. More than that and then wham…

*(**LYNN** demonstrates a hard, powerful kick, high into the air.)*

Right through all of them into the net! Beautiful.

NANCY. *(modestly)* Yeah, well. Figured it was now or never, right?

(They smile and wave toward the field, each standing very still. Their last lines do not overlap.)

NANCY. JACK!

ALISON. AARON, SWEETIE, GO TELL DAD WE CAN GO HOME NOW!

LYNN. LARRY! LARRY, YOUR WATER BOTTLE!…NO, I'M NOT GETTING IT. YOU GET IT!

NANCY. JACK, COME ON…WHAT, HONEY?…THANK YOU. YOU PLAYED A GREAT GAME TOO…WHAT DO YOU SAY WE GO OUT AND CELEBRATE?

(The three women take one last look at one another, smile, then exit as the rock and roll anthem from the prologue begins to play.)

(BLACK OUT)

End of Play

PROPS

Set:
Large rectangle canvas painted blue with white cumulus clouds
Autumn leaves
2 backless park benches or short bleachers
Park garbage can/lid optional
3 small rolling tables and 3 radios *(for prologue)*

Alison:
Sport bag
Sport bottle
Cell phone
Towel
"Soccer for Dummies" book
Soccer ball
Tissue
Small paper with "married couple" joke
Suitcase and clothes for packing, including negligee (for prologue)

Lynn:
Large canvas tote bag
Large 3-ring binder ofPTA work
Wet wipes
Cell phone
Day planner
Chair cushion
Kids pencil box with pens and highlighters
One copy of "The Happy Man and His Dump Truck"

Large envelope labeled "Good Night Moon"
Large black marker
Envelopes, order forms, marker and Little Golden Books (for prologue)

Nancy:
Large black purse
Water bottle
35 mm camera
Cell phone
Small bottle of aspirin
Sport ice pack
Case with rolls of film
Laundry basket filled with white clothes (for prologue)

COSTUMES

Alison:
Sport sunglasses with strap
Head and wrist bands
Zip-up sweatshirt (long sleeve with hood)
Tee shirt
Sport top
Short bike shorts
Track suit pants
White sport socks
Cross trainer sneakers

Lynn:
Sweater (wool, zip-up, no hood)
Short-sleeve tee shirt
Light denim jeans
Keds sneakers
White socks
Glasses

Nancy:
Stylish sunglasses
Black pants or jeans
Black turtleneck
Stylish fall jacket or wrap
Black socks
Black leather running shoes

From the Reviews of
SECRETS OF A SOCCER MOM...

"Let's hear it for *Secrets of A Soccer Mom,* a diverting new comedy by
Kathleen Clark."
- *The New York Times*

"A sympathetic and compelling comedy with constant laughs."
- *Variety*

"Soccer moms of the world, unite and jog over to enjoy Kathleen
Clark's new comedy."
- *Associated Press*

"*Secrets of A Soccer Mom* puts the heart and 'sole' into comedy."
- *New York Daily News*

Also by
Kathleen Clark...

Southern Comforts

Please visit our website **samuelfrench.com** for complete
descriptions and licensing information

OTHER TITLES AVAILABLE FROM SAMUEL FRENCH

THE SCENE
Theresa Rebeck

Little Theatre / Drama / 2m, 2f / Interior Unit Set
A young social climber leads an actor into an extra-marital affair, from which he then creates a full-on downward spiral into alcoholism and bummery. His wife runs off with his best friend, his girlfriend leaves, and he's left with... nothing.

"Ms. Rebeck's dark-hued morality tale contains enough fresh insights into the cultural landscape to freshen what is essentially a classic boy-meets-bad-girl story."
- New York Times

"Rebeck's wickedly scathing observations about the sort of self-obsessed New Yorkers who pursue their own interests at the cost of their morality and loyalty."
- New York Post

"The Scene is utterly delightful in its comedic performances, and its slowly unraveling plot is thought-provoking and gut-wrenching."
- Show Business Weekly